by
Rachel Ruiz

illustrated by
Melissa Manwill

When **Penny** Met
POTUS

CAPSTONE YOUNG READERS
a Capstone imprint

Today is going to be Penny's best day ever.

Why?

Because today she's going to work with her mom!

Penny's mom has a very important job at a big white house. Her boss's name is POTUS. Isn't that a funny name?

You say it like this:

POE-TUS.
Silly, right?

POE-
TUS

Penny hasn't met
POTUS yet, but she
imagines what he
might look like.

Penny knows POTUS must be really special because he has his own team of secret service agents.

They protect POTUS anytime,
anyplace — even in outer space.

POTUS also has his own airplane
to take him wherever he needs to
go and a personal chef to make
him delicious POTUS sandwiches.

Penny practices what she will say if she ever gets to meet POTUS.

Your Majesty, it is an honor.

POTUS will invite her back to his house.

They will have a tea party.

POTUS will ask Penny to help
with some important work.

It will be amazing.

As soon as they arrive at her mom's office,
Penny asks, "When can I meet POTUS?"

"Maybe later," her mom
says. "I have to make
a few calls first."

Penny tries to be patient,
but she simply can't wait
another minute.

She tiptoes out of her mom's
office and sets out to find
POTUS on her own.

The big white house is bustling with busy people going about their work. Maybe one of them can help Penny find POTUS.

"Excuse me, sir," Penny says. "Have you seen POTUS?"

The man shakes his head.
"Not since I brought in the morning paper and coffee."

"Excuse me, ma'am," Penny says.
"Have you seen POTUS?"

The woman shakes her head.

"Not since yesterday. POTUS likes
to sit here and smell the roses."

"Excuse me, ma'am," Penny
says. "Have you seen POTUS?"

"As a matter of fact,"
the woman says, "I have."

"You have?" Penny asks.
"Where?"

"Penny, there you are!" her mom says.
"I've been looking for you everywhere!"

"I'm sorry, Mom. I didn't mean to make you worry.
I just wanted to find POTUS," Penny explains.

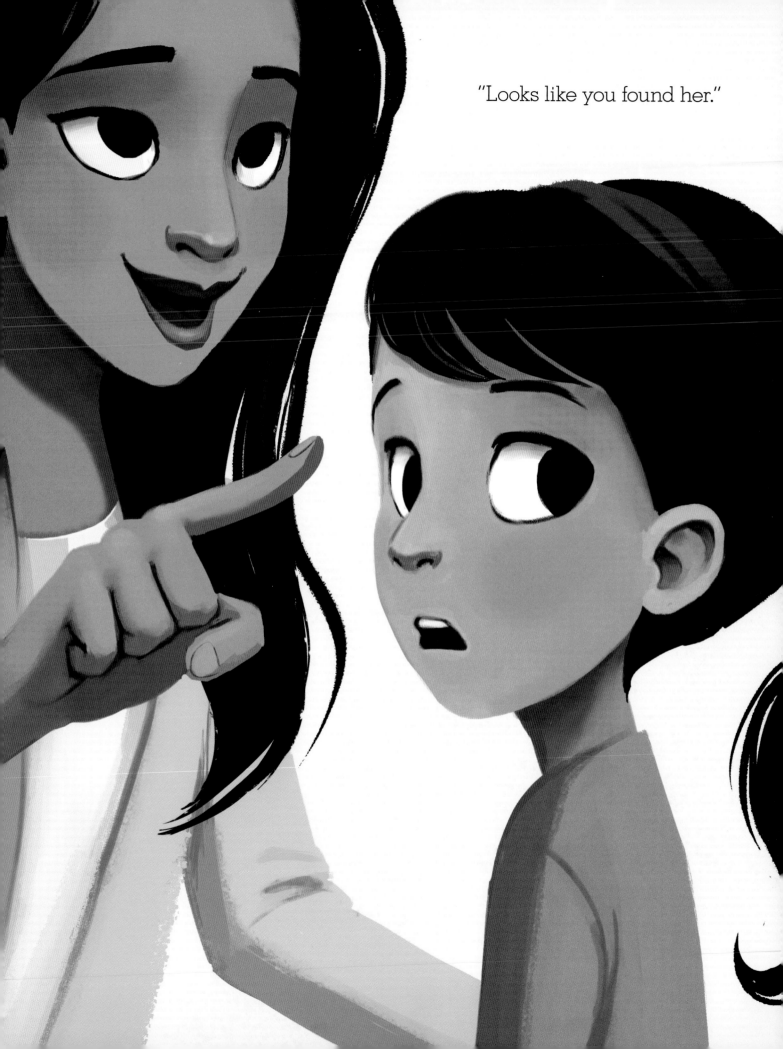

"Looks like you found her."

Penny looks at the woman.

"You're POTUS?"

The woman nods, smiling.
"POTUS is a nickname people use
for me," she says. "It stands for
President of the United States."

"You're the president?" Penny asks.
"But you're a —"

"Human," Penny says.

She feels a little disappointed.

But that disappointment turns into excitement when Penny realizes that POTUS is a lot like her.

In fact, it gets her thinking . . .
Penny for POTUS?

She sure likes the sound of that!

To Macy

Thank you for your relentless curiosity
and your boundless imagination — R.R.

When Penny Met POTUS is published by
Capstone Young Readers, a Capstone imprint
1710 Roe Crest Drive, North Mankato, Minnesota 56003
www.mycapstone.com

Text copyright © 2016 Rachel Ruiz
Illustrations copyright © 2016 Capstone Young Readers

Library of Congress Cataloging-in-Publication Data
Names: Ruiz, Rachel (Rachel Marie), author. | Manwill, Melissa, illustrator.
Title: When Penny met POTUS / by Rachel Ruiz ; illustrated by Melissa Manwill.
Description: North Mankato, Minnesota: Picture Window Books, a Capstone imprint, [2016]
Summary: Penny knows that her mother works for somebody called the POTUS, but she does
not know what that means, and the odd name seems to her to imply some kind of friendly monster.
Identifiers: LCCN 2016007951| ISBN 9781515802181 (library binding) | ISBN 9781623707583 (paper over board) |
ISBN 9781515802198 (ebook pdf) Subjects: LCSH: Imagination—Juvenile fiction. | Presidents—United States—Juvenile fiction. |
CYAC: Presidents—Fiction. | Imagination—Fiction. | Monsters—Fiction. Classification: LCC PZ7.1.R85 Wh 2016 | DDC [E]—dc23
LC record available at http://lccn.loc.gov/2016007951

Jacket and book design by Bob Lentz

Printed in China.
009577F16